ECHOES OF BLOOD

Pablo Roy Leguisamo

Copyright © 2024 Pablo Leguísamo

All rights reserved. Reproduction, distribution, or transmission of this work, in whole or in part, in any form or by any means, without the written permission of the author, is strictly prohibited.

Any similarities to real events, persons, or places are purely coincidental and the result of the author's imagination.

ISBN: 9798329020137

CONTENTS

Title Page

Copyright

Foreword

I	1
II	6
III	11
IV	17
V	21
VI	25
VII	30
VIII	35
IX	40
X	45
XI	53
XII	59
XIII	63
XIV	69

XV	76
XVI	81
XVII	87
XVIII	92
XIX	96
XX	102
XXI	106
XXII	111
XXIII	116
EPILOGUE	119
II	123
About The Author	127

FOREWORD

In the 1960s, an armed group called the Tupamaros rose against the government in Uruguay, engaging in acts of urban guerrilla warfare and significant political activism. Many members were imprisoned during the struggle.

By the early 21st century, several former Tupamaros had transitioned into politics. In 2010, José "Pepe" Mujica, a prominent leader of the group, was elected President of Uruguay.

I

The funeral parlor was nearly empty. Carolina's heels echoed in the room, drawing the attention of the few attendees. She would have stood out anyway; she was the only person under 40 in the room, and her suggestive miniskirt made her legs a visual escape for the mourners. No one knew her; she was a stranger entering what seemed like a private club. Some stopped ogling her thighs to notice the small recorder she held; their looks shifted from lust to accusation in moments. "Who does this chick think she is, coming here?" "Journalists have no respect anymore." "What they do to sell a few more newspapers, shameful." Carolina felt the disapproval from each of the former guerrillas bidding farewell to Ricardo "El Ruso" Yanquelevich.

According to the police report, gunshots had been heard throughout the block. The neighborhood ladies woke up at two-thirty in the morning, frightened by the bangs followed by the cacophony of barking dogs in the area.

"He was a good person, they called him the old Russian. Sometimes he'd buy pastries for the neighborhood kids, and until a few years ago, he'd join in the soccer games down at the field," the evening news had made an effort to show the victim's personal side in their human interest segment. However, the news anchor emphasized that this was the third ex-Tupamaro murdered in the last four years. Although there was no official confirmation—the police spokesperson had avoided commenting on it—the murder was linked to the group responsible for the previous attacks.

The next day, the newsroom of the daily newspaper buzzed with excitement. Carolina imagined this was how her professors must have lived, talking so much about "scoops," "deadlines," and "press runs," when people waited for the newspaper to be informed, not when the newspaper waited to reach at least two thousand readers to cover printing costs. She forced herself to abandon that line of thought because she knew it would end with: "if she had studied journalism to write an article about what color underwear women wear during Nostalgia Night."

In the editorial meeting, it was clear that El Ruso's murder would take precedence over any other news or ongoing investigation. The popularity of the Tupamaros in Uruguay and internationally, combined with the figure of a former guerrilla president and the possibility of the reappearance of a group seeking retribution through violence, provided a golden opportunity to sell newspapers. Not to mention the chance—present but silent, being a press outlet linked to a right-wing group—of obtaining some past information that could tarnish the image of the Tupamaros turned politicians, especially with elections so close.

"Aguirre, you go to the wake and see if you can dig up something there," Carolina's expression betrayed her lack of interest. Just when she could investigate a crime report, she was assigned the emotional story. "Look for juicy details; an ex-girlfriend, a grudge with one of his comrades, family members he may have left behind due to his activism."

From there, Carolina continued on autopilot. Wake, filler story, and waiting for something more interesting to happen in her career.

"Do you think you can come here and take advantage of the situation? What yellow rag are you working for?" A man with a prominent beard and belly stopped in front of her. He pulled out an iPhone from his jacket and typed fervently. "Come on, tell me. I want to speak to your boss. Tell me, sweetheart!"

Several attendees crowded around the only sign of life in the room, but it was a newcomer who intervened.

"Young lady, this is not how things are done. There's a protocol for these kinds of stories; they should have taught you that," the sermon came from a tall man with long hair who looked much younger than the others. Carolina recognized him, but his name escaped her; he was one of the many political figures gaining media prominence before the elections.

"Pitito, stay out of this." Pitito! Wilton "El Pitito" Motta. Carolina suddenly remembered how the campaign advisor had repeatedly called the newsroom to implore them to avoid using his client's nickname in the articles. And more than one wondered if Motta hadn't earned the nickname while the Tupamaros shared time in prison. "Get out of here before you make things worse!"

"Hey, Benteveo, you're going overboard," Pitito responded.

Furious, the bearded man pushed the girl aside and shoved Motta into a corner. No one remembered the open casket resting a few meters away anymore. The entrance to the room was a hubbub of reproaches and shoving matches among sexagenarians, with the bearded man and Motta at its center, seemingly about to come to blows. Carolina didn't want to miss anything; if she couldn't secure an interview, at least she would have material for a story about the chaos at the wake. A stocky man in a gray suit and sunglasses pulled Pitito away from the argument, while bony fingers grabbed her arm and dragged her out of the room. She tried to resist to witness the outcome, but moments later, she was already downstairs.

"It's best if you leave," the man, gaunt with thick gray hair and a neatly trimmed beard peppered with gray, escorted her (now more gently) towards the exit door. "I wouldn't want you to leave with a bad impression of El Ruso, or those who cared for him. What happened here was..."

"Excuse me, but who are you?" Carolina's diplomacy was about to run out.

"A friend of El Ruso, they call me the Astute."

II

The water was near freezing. The pipe serving as a shower spewed a thick stream that struck the Astute's naked body with force. Out in the open, in the courtyard and at the mercy of the winds coming from the coast, showering in Punta Carretas Prison required a lot of willpower. The Astute turned off the faucet and reached out, feeling for the towel.

He had been transferred to the prison just a few days ago and, after the torture, beatings, and starvation, he thought he would appreciate the change. However, the Astute was one of the first guerrillas moved to the prison on Ellauri Street, and the adjustment was proving more difficult than expected.

"Don't leave, skinny, come on, we don't bite," a man with a mustache and a strange scar on his ear was undressing in the next shower. Behind him, two more inmates blocked the way, one of them grinning from ear to ear, showing the only tooth he had left.

The Astute turned the faucet back on, and the stream of icy water made his shower companions retreat. He moved a few steps away, grabbed his clothes, and headed back to his cell, hearing the laughter coming from the showers.

Days passed, and the bruises from the torture were now showing a healthy greenish color. He cautiously tried to ask some inmates about other guerrillas, other Tupamaros in the prison, but that only seemed to make him even more vulnerable.

The spoon moved among pieces of who-knows-what. The Astute stirred the mush to find something recognizable as food. The dining hall was full, but he sat alone, unsure even of starting a conversation.

"You know, we have some smuggled food if you're having trouble with that slop," a tall, dark-skinned man with a Brazilian accent sat next to him. Another man, dressed only in shorts despite the cold, stood behind the first.

"And you're just going to give it to me?"

"Don't be stupid, I think you know what we want in return." The Astute swallowed a spoonful of the gray mush and didn't reply. The Brazilian frowned and left the table; his companion grabbed his crotch over his shorts and blew a kiss at the Astute before leaving him alone with his plate of food.

The encounter with the Brazilian left him uneasy, and he spent the following days holed up in his cell. He took short walks, just to stretch his legs a bit and see if he could find any comrades. But inside the small room, he felt safe, especially if his cellmate was there. The "Yugoslav," as he had heard him called, only knew a few words of Spanish and spent most of his time lying on the cot with his eyes closed. He didn't quite know why, but that presence brought him a sense of peace.

That afternoon, the Yugoslav got up at the sound of the five o'clock bells and left the cell. The Astute, absorbed in his reading, didn't notice until the metal door slammed shut for the second time, making him look up. The Brazilian approached with a blade in his hand, while his companion—leaning against the door, now without his shorts—was fondling himself expectantly.

The tall man received a book to the nose with full force and retaliated with a deep cut to the leg. The Astute clutched his thigh and felt the blood as the Brazilian pounced on him. He struggled futilely until his face was pressed against the wall, feeling heavy breathing on his neck. With a yank, his pants were ripped off. The Astute kicked rebelliously but only managed to make the Brazilian press the knife against his throat.

"Come on, hurry up, you coward!" he shouted, knowing he was defeated.

The tall man unbuttoned his pants. The bulky figure pressed against the scrawny Tupamaro, who clenched his teeth in anticipation. Behind them, there was a thud, and after a guttural sound, the Astute felt a warm liquid soaking his back.

"You can turn around now," said a man with broad shoulders and thick arms, holding a bloody knife. The guy in the shorts lay on the ground with his head bashed in, and the Brazilian was writhing as a trickle of blood flowed from his throat. "And put your pants on."

After that, the Astute felt only tranquility. A sensation that didn't fade even when he had to drag the bodies to an empty cell and spend hours scrubbing the floor and cleaning the bloodstains, nor when he waited for a possible call from the guards, which never came.

From that moment on, with a companion by his side, he was able to endure everything differently. Together, they prepared the ground for the next Tupamaros who would inevitably arrive in the months and years to come. The Astute never forgot how he met him, not when they left the prison, nor when the dictatorship ended. Because that was El Ruso for him, the guy who watched his back.

III

The electric kettle clicked, signaling the water was boiling. The Astute got up from the bed and carried the radio to the kitchen. He crossed the few meters of his one-bedroom apartment, where he had lived for 20 years. It never seemed strange to him that after spending so much time in a tiny cell, he chose to live in a small place without a balcony or large windows, where everything was within reach. He would say he didn't need anything more, that being able to drink some mate while sitting at the small kitchen table, looking at a piece of sky and listening to the radio, was enough.

The station was replaying—once again—the latest interview with President José Mujica. Fate had it that the guerrillas were now in government, enjoying popularity once more, but this time without violence, without weapons, and without fear. The Astute always maintained a low profile, and his refusal to participate in politics had been unequivocal. "Not interested," he had said to end the matter once and for all.

The interviewer inquired about the murder of his former comrade and the possibility that it was the resurgence of revenge attacks. Mujica lamented the loss of El Ruso, reinforced his confidence in the police forces and the Interior Minister (whom he "fully supported"), then diverged into a story about a farm in China. He ended with a strange metaphor that veered away from the topic but left the journalist satisfied.

The intercom buzzed from the tiny living room.

Why had he agreed to an interview after staying silent for so many years? He wasn't Mujica and didn't like talking to journalists; he had avoided them so thoroughly, yet now...

"Yes?"

"Carolina Aguirre."

"Come on up." The Astute took those moments to tidy up a few things in the room and dust the table with his forearm.

"Do you mind if I put the recorder here?" The girl

extended her hand and placed the device a few inches from the Astute.

"No, it's fine," he said, trying to hide his discomfort. "Do you want a mate?"

"Were you and El Ruso close?" Carolina reached out for the drink.

"Very close friends," the Astute rubbed his face in regret. "We had drifted apart, but after what happened a few months ago..."

"What happened a few months ago? The murders? The armed group?"

"No. El Ruso was having money problems..." The Astute paused for a few seconds to gather his thoughts. "He had distanced himself from the group several years ago and wasn't interested in politics. In that, we were similar, but he was more..."

"Come here, you son of a bitch! You motherfucker!" The white garden chair crashed against the red flag hanging on the wall. El Ruso, nearly sixty years old, leaped over a makeshift table to punch one of the leaders giving a speech. The tensions in the committee had been high since the beginning of the meeting, but now more than six sexagenarians were struggling to pull El Ruso off his victim. The Astute repressed the memory.

"Intense?" she handed back the mate with a smile.

"That's one way to put it," the Astute continued. "I'm not sure how it started, but after the Pepe Mujica boom, they offered him to write a book."

"About him?" she interrupted.

"About him, the movement, the time we spent in prison; anything they could turn into a bestseller."

"That's not unusual. There have been a lot of books like that in recent years."

"That's true," the Astute sipped his mate and counted to three, struggling enough with this without being interrupted every five seconds. "But El Ruso made it clear he didn't want the board to review the book before sending it to the publisher. Many distanced themselves from him, and quite a few cut ties altogether. Later on, he told me how hard it had been to get any of the comrades to agree to be interviewed for the book, and I had no choice but to lend him a hand..."

"But that argument at the wake?"

"Well, Pitito... Motta didn't like the idea. In fact, he was the first to refuse to participate, and his campaign office raised the request for the book to be 'reviewed.'" The Astute met Carolina's gaze; her eyes sparkled at the information she had in her grasp. "But that's not why I agreed to this interview. I wanted to give you a more realistic picture of El Ruso, beyond the political scandals."

"And what was he like?"

"He was a good man," he looked towards the bookshelf, where almost hidden among the many books, was a small unframed photo. Three men in their forties smiled on a beach in Colonia del Sacramento. The only photo he had with El Ruso and Benteveo. "The kind you always want by your side..."

The Astute's voice broke; it was the first time he had truly acknowledged the loss of El Ruso, that there would be no more late-night whiskies reminiscing about old times.

"Forgive me," he said, under the astonished gaze of the young journalist who seemed never to have seen an ex-guerrilla cry. "I just can't believe they killed him."

"But this isn't the first attack by these people, and they never caught them."

"The R.G.? I don't think it was them. It can't be."

"Why are you so sure?"

"Because El Ruso never fired a single shot during the whole guerrilla campaign."

IV

A thunderclap had woken her at five in the morning, and by the time Carolina left for work, she knew what awaited her: puddles, loose tiles, and overcrowded buses. Walking three blocks in the pouring rain and arriving at the office with soaked feet had extinguished the last of her good humor.

She greeted the newspaper's doorman with a nod and grabbed a copy of the morning edition from the hall. She squeezed into the elevator with five other people but managed to open the paper and skim through the articles.

"Unbelievable! For fuck's sake!" Several disapproving glances shot her way.

The article about El Ruso's funeral hadn't been published. Instead, there was a review of a graphic novel from six months ago. Carolina's irritation quickly turned to fury. The story she'd worked on all week, the only moderately interesting assignment she'd had since starting at the paper, and a piece of solid journalism to boot, was nowhere to be found. How could this have happened? As she stormed up the stairs to the editorial office, she thought of reasons that might calm her down, and there were very few.

Before barging into the editor's office, Carolina collided with a short man in sunglasses who greeted her politely. She barely noticed him. She stood in front of her boss, and didn't need to say a word.

"I know, I know..." said the man, now looking smaller behind his desk. "It wasn't my decision, and it was out of my hands. It came from above..."

Carolina's expression changed. This wasn't one of the explanations she'd anticipated, and she couldn't quite grasp what had happened.

"You have to understand, Aguirre," he continued, gesturing for her to sit. "We're close to the elections... you know how it is..."

"No, I don't. Explain it to me."

"The order came from above. I don't know what favors were called in, but since yesterday afternoon we've been getting calls from Wilton Motta's campaign headquarters, and eventually, one of the directors asked us not to run the piece. I protested as much as I could..."

"Clearly not enough," Carolina said, crossing her arms defiantly. "Give me one reason not to take this story to another paper."

"And you think this won't happen at another place? Don't be naive, Aguirre. Between the return of the Reparation Group..."

"Possible return," she interrupted. "No one has confirmed this is another attack by the R.G."

"Fine, whatever, but between that and the elections, they're working overtime to keep dirty laundry from airing. I'm sorry, it shouldn't happen, but what can you do?"

Carolina fell silent. There was nothing to say; she was disappointed and had no chance of winning a fight she'd already lost the day before.

"Anyway..." the editor's tone softened, trying to sound more conciliatory. "Motta wanted to make it up to you for any trouble caused."

Carolina raised an eyebrow.

"He offered you an exclusive interview," he

continued. "In fact, his campaign coordinator just left to arrange it."

"Can I ask whatever I want and be sure it'll be published?"

He didn't answer, but they both knew the response.

V

"Green first, cracked on top, silver below, thick at the back; green first, cracked on top, silver below, thick at the back." The Astute repeated the phrase to keep his mind off the unpleasant task awaiting him six bus stops away.

The cursed route he had taken was filled with memories. He'd never thought of it that way, but the bus seemed to pass only by places that reminded him of El Ruso. Maybe it was because all the neighborhood bars were on that avenue, and the long chats and heated debates were now playing out before his eyes. He forced himself to discard the thought. "Green first..."

One thing was clear: the loss of El Ruso had affected him more than he wanted to admit. It seemed increasingly unlikely this was an attack by the Reparation Group, leaving him with more questions. Why kill him at home? He had always imagined that one morning he would read about El Ruso's death resulting from some brawl in a dark corner of Montevideo, thanks to his knack for riling up drinking companions. But at home? It hadn't been a robbery; the police had dismissed that theory immediately.

He walked up to the metal door, and suddenly, the task he had been postponing for the past week became real and immediate. There was no escaping it: he had to do it. It wasn't the most horrible job the Astute had done, but it was certainly the most painful.

"Green first," he repeated aloud as he inserted the key with the green head into the lock.

The hallway was dark even at midday.

"You pay nearly a thousand pesos in expenses, and they don't change the light bulb? Why don't you complain?"

"It's a bit dark, but it keeps the mood when I bring a girl over," El Ruso's words echoed loudly in his mind.

"Cracked on top, silver below," the Astute continued reciting Mrs. Yanquelevich's words.

The door opened, and the room was just as he remembered it from the last time he had seen

El Ruso. El Ruso had been busy and very excited about his book. Returning to writing and research had done him a lot of good. Like many other ex-guerrillas, El Ruso had struggled to continue with his life after the years in prison. After two failed marriages, El Ruso's mother was the only family he had left. Mrs. Yanquelevich had been like a mother to many militants; she had hidden, cared for, and fed them during the worst times and even conveyed vital messages for guerrilla operations. Now, at ninety-five years old, the least the Astute could do for her was to take care of her son's belongings and get the small rented apartment in shape to hand it back to the owners, which included cleaning up the crime scene.

The Astute took a deep breath, climbed the narrow stairs, and walked down the hallway to the room El Ruso used as a study. He pushed the door open and heard a noise nearby. He didn't notice the bloodstain on the floor or the red splatters on the bookshelf; what caught his attention first was the lit-up laptop. Another noise. This time, he knew it came from the patio. The window in the room was slightly open, the lock had been forced. Three meters below, in the patio, he saw a figure getting ready to climb the wall.

He ran downstairs and stopped in front of the kitchen door. He pulled the bunch of keys from his pocket and cursed under his breath.

"Which one was it?" His shaky hands inspected them one by one. "The thick one for the back."

He stepped out into the patio and saw the intruder climbing onto the roof of the neighboring house. The Astute ran and scaled the wall, jumped into the neighbor's yard, and tried to mimic the movements of the young man he was chasing. His gnarled fingers gripped the rooftop, and he managed to pull himself up but had to pause to catch his breath. He looked up and saw a red cap and cursive letters tattooed on a neck a few meters away. But by the time he regained his strength, the thief had already jumped back down to the street and was running away down one of the side streets.

"Damn, how I wish I were thirty years younger..."

VI

"The nose looks strange. And what's that spot there?"

"Don't worry, all that will be fixed later with Photoshop." The cursor moved across the screen, erasing some imperfections and subtly changing the skin tone in the photo.

"That's much better."

"See? I told you not to worry. The photoshoot went very well. You'll see how great the posters turn out." The short man patted the girl sitting behind the computer on the back and guided Pitito Motta out of the room. "Come on, let them work."

After a series of handshakes and greetings, Motta and his campaign manager left the advertising agency. Pitito was still fixated on how strange his nose looked in the photographs when his phone vibrated.

"Karen, tell me..." Motta sighed heavily. "Oh, yes... I completely forgot... no, no, tell her to wait for me in the conference room. I'll be there in... ten minutes. Thanks."

The manager looked at him curiously.

"The blonde, I forgot we scheduled the interview for today." The man beside him still seemed confused about whom he was referring to. "The one about the funeral piece. This never seems to end."

"The worst is over. Get rid of the girl quickly and forget about it. I have to go to Rodríguez's place for the event in Florida and then I'll head to the office."

The small man put on his sunglasses and walked away. Motta stood still, deep in thought, as if the call had opened a file he preferred to keep hidden.

"Mariño, wait!" Motta suddenly shouted. The campaign manager turned back, and Pitito spoke to him in a low voice. "Did you take care of the other thing?"

"I'll confirm in a bit, but don't worry. I told you I'd handle it."

✼ ✼ ✼

The meeting room was a glass cubicle. Except for the side with the majestic view of Rodó Park, the other translucent walls faced the office interior. Motta had requested curtains several months ago, but the urgencies of the campaign postponed the purchase. "The fishbowl," as the staff called it, allowed everyone to gauge the mood and tone of private meetings. The future senator disliked it, but it provided constant entertainment for the office.

When Motta arrived, the fishbowl had only one occupant, a blonde woman who seemed impatient and very annoyed. Pitito knew he had to get through this, and it was best to do it quickly, like ripping off a band-aid.

"Karen, could you bring us two coffees?" he said as he walked toward the glass cage.

"Sorry for the delay," Motta said, taking a seat on the other side of the table.

"That's not what I'm waiting for you to apologize for," Carolina said, taking the recorder out of her bag and placing it, turned on, on the table.

Motta swallowed hard. He hadn't expected such a confrontational attitude, and he didn't have Mariño to bail him out.

"Let's start the interview, please." Pitito kept his

composure, clasped his hands on the table, and waited for the first question.

"Fine by me," Carolina smiled. "Mr. Motta, what are you trying so hard to hide that you pressured the newspaper where I work not to publish the article about Ricardo Yanquelevich's funeral?"

The man stared at her and then noticed the red light on the recorder.

"I don't know what you're talking about."

"You know, I didn't study journalism for this. I don't know if it's because I'm a woman, I'm young, or what, but either way, I don't like being taken for a fool."

Pitito reached for the recorder and pressed the "stop" button.

"Look, I have nothing against you, but you have to understand how this works. There are interests, people who have invested money... that's how politics works."

"I thought politics was supposed to function with integrity."

Through the glass of the fishbowl, Motta saw Mariño enter the office and signaled for him to come over.

The short man trotted to the meeting room.

"Wilton, what you asked for is done," he said as he opened the door. "And don't forget your meeting in fifteen minutes."

"You don't need to make excuses, Motta, I'm leaving," Carolina stood up. "Fortunately, today there are more ways for people to get the news."

"Don't make me talk to your editor again," Mariño threatened.

Carolina ignored the comment and left the office.

"Do you want me to call the newspaper?"

"I don't know what I want..." Motta held his head and gazed out at the city and the darkness beginning to loom on the horizon.

VII

The tall grass reached up to his waist. He walked carefully; the area was treacherous, and one wrong step could mean drowning in one of the many stagnant pools of water around. The light was fading, and nightfall was imminent. The Astute knew that if he didn't reach the rendezvous point within the next hour, navigating the wetland would be impossible. He wasn't exactly sure where he was going—the information he'd received was scant and cryptic, even for the Tupamaros—but if the content and the sender were real, he had no choice but to push forward.

Forty-five minutes later, with soaked feet, he arrived at a clearing. There, he saw a structure made of wood and sheet metal. If that wasn't the place, at least he could dry off and rest before continuing the search. He knocked, and the door swung open on its own.

"We've been expecting you."
"Lost your way, Astute?"

The three men sitting around a small gas lantern stood up to greet him. It had been a while since they'd seen each other: after the defeat and the Coup, their meetings had been sporadic and only in cases of dire necessity. Clandestinity was routine, which was why the Astute had hesitated so much before leaving his hiding place.

"I'm not sure if this is a time for jokes," the Astute said, moving to the center of the neglected room. "Are we all here?"

"Only El Ruso is missing," a man with long blonde sideburns stepped closer to the light. "We thought he might come with you."

"I haven't seen him in a while," the Astute lamented. "I'm afraid he might have fallen again."

On the other side of the lantern, Pitito shuddered at the idea that seemed to confirm his fears. Sitting next to him on the same wooden crate, the Benteveo, now much plumper than the Astute remembered, pulled a gun from his pants.

"Maca heard that the military might come for us," Benteveo remarked, pointing at the blonde.

There was a click as Benteveo released the revolver's cylinder and checked that it was loaded.

"Take this," he handed the gun to the newcomer. "Knowing you, you didn't bring one with you. You need to be armed in case they come for us."

Benteveo was right on both counts.

They spent thirty-five minutes in silence. They were hidden in an unknown location, but they feared even the reeds might be listening. Suddenly, a splash startled them. Benteveo drew his weapon and aimed it at the door. Pitito hid behind some bags of dirt, and Maca dimmed the lantern.

A face peered through a crack. The Astute was the first to recognize it.

"Ruso!" He pulled him into the rickety structure with a hug.

The danger of being discovered didn't prevent them from enjoying the meager food amidst laughter and memories of the days they shared in Punta Carretas Prison. The Astute hadn't brought a weapon, but he had packed some canned goods; years of hiding and living in secrecy had taught him that hunger always made things seem worse.

* * *

Inside, they slept. The structure was silent. Outside, Maca and Benteveo kept watch over the area. Pistol in hand, Benteveo thought he heard a conversation and approached to investigate.

The Astute woke to the second gunshot. The Tupamaros scrambled for cover amid the shouts and gunfire. Bullets whizzed overhead, leaving holes in the sheet metal walls. El Ruso made an opening at the back of the structure and pushed Pitito and the Astute through.

"Let's go, we have to get out of here!"

"Where's Benteveo?" Pitito exclaimed. "We can't leave him."

The Astute could see Benteveo's silhouette running in the distance, but there was no sign of Maca. Pitito moved to go after Benteveo, but El Ruso stopped him.

"Don't be stupid. Keep your head down and follow me."

The three ran between the trees, feeling the flashlights and the shouts of the soldiers at their backs. They were about to reach the top of a small hill that ended in a ravine, but Pitito stumbled, and in helping him up, they lost all the advantage they had gained.

"Stop right there!"

The lights blinded Motta, who shielded his face with his hands. El Ruso stepped back and grabbed the Astute by the shirt.

"You already got stuck in Punta Carretas," he said, pushing him down the slope.

The Astute couldn't react. He rolled several times and ended up in a dense thicket. He had a bump on his head, and his right arm was out of place, but he endured the pain and circled the area to find out what had happened to his comrades. He hid behind a huge tree trunk and watched as they beat Pitito and El Ruso and shoved them into the back of a truck. He couldn't see Benteveo, but he could distinguish Maca. He squinted to confirm it. There was no doubt; he was sitting in the car next to one of the soldiers.

VIII

He reached into the back of the compartment, feeling around for some books and a shoebox. He pulled everything toward him, the chair wobbling as he lost his balance. Two thick hands caught him.

"You're gonna kill yourself, you idiot," said Benteveo, grabbing the Astute and helping him carefully climb down. "Consider yourself lucky, as long as you're all skin and bones, someone can catch you in midair."

The Astute smiled and responded with a hearty hug.

"You left the door open," Benteveo said, jumping up and grabbing the books and the dusty box with a swift motion.

"Thanks for coming to give me a hand."

El Ruso's closet had kept the Astute busy all

morning. The endless books, which had already filled the living room and study shelves, still occupied several additional shelves. Then there was the pile of clothes to donate and the souvenirs from his travels across Latin America. Everything had been a challenge, but nothing as much as what lay in the box now resting on his lap.

"Damn, I didn't remember being this young," the Astute said, picking up one of the many photographs and showing it to Benteveo.

"I didn't remember being this skinny," Benteveo replied, stroking the large belly protruding from his torso.

What started as a quick and efficient job slowed down suddenly, and now the two of them were sitting, contemplating the pile of rectangular memories they had uncovered. Beneath the photos of unknown relatives, they found a stack of pictures of themselves, some even from before the dictatorship (which they couldn't believe hadn't been burned at the time) and others they had never seen before.

The Astute was mesmerized, staring at a photo of three men on a beach. Written on the back in pen, it said, "El Lechón, the Astute, and me at Punta Espinillo." The Astute wasn't smiling; he looked annoyed. Why couldn't he remember that moment? What year was it? It frustrated him that his memory could be so tangled.

"Look at this one!" Benteveo grabbed a photo from the bottom. "Do you remember?"

1987, Santa Teresa campground. The Astute, El Ruso, Pitito, Benteveo, Vasquito, Maca, Lechón, Raquel, Peti, and several other comrades—one of the last times they were all together. After that, they only met at funerals.

"A shame that traitor is in it."

The photo fell onto the pile the Astute was sorting to keep. Maca's betrayal had never been clear. The lack of evidence and the fragmented memories of those present meant the case never advanced beyond a superficial investigation. However, for some comrades, what was known was more than enough.

"Come on, Bente, don't be like that. We were never sure..."

"That cowardly bastard? A sellout," Benteveo grabbed a large stack of books and left the room.

The floorboards creaked.

"I think four is the maximum."

Benteveo placed the crate of books on the floor.

"Luckily, this is the last one..."

The living room was now a giant Jenga, and the two had to squeeze between piles of book crates to take a break.

"Here, it's a bit cold, but it'll do."

"Did you report it?" Benteveo reached out for the mate.

"No, what for?"

"What's wrong with you? Don't you trust our police force?" he said, sipping hard from the straw.

"It was nothing, they didn't steal anything..." the Astute looked at the laptop on the coffee table. "It's over..."

"What if that guy was the one who killed him? You said yourself it looked like he was checking something on the computer..." Benteveo stood up and handed back the mate. "Anything can help the investigation."

"Yeah, I don't know..." the Astute focused on adjusting the straw.

"Don't you want to catch those Reparation Group bastards?" Benteveo didn't back down and stood in front of the Astute.

"I don't think it was them. Not El Ruso..."

"If not them, then who?" Benteveo couldn't believe what he was hearing. "They probably have no idea what each of us did, just that we were involved. They're picking us off like flies."

The Astute lowered his head and prepared another mate.

"Look, I know all this is hard..." Benteveo's thick fingers squeezed his friend's shoulder. "Do you want to give me the laptop, and I'll report it? You don't have to do everything yourself."

The Astute hesitated. He didn't want to go to the police station, but he couldn't shake the feeling that everything rested on him. If there was even a small chance to catch El Ruso's killer, he had to take it.

"No, leave it. I'll handle it."

IX

She hadn't heard the alarm and missed the bus. Carolina hurried to the newspaper offices only to find the elevator under repair. The stairs drained what little breath and energy she had left to face the day. When she peeked into the newsroom, she was met with silence. Some of her colleagues looked at her with surprise, while others avoided eye contact. Carolina greeted them with a general "hello" that didn't expect a response and headed to her cubicle. Only after tossing her purse onto the table did she realize someone else was occupying that workspace. She looked around as if searching for an answer, but she didn't need one; it was clear what was happening, and tact was scarce in that workplace.

She walked determinedly to her ex-boss's office and pushed the door wide open.

"I hope they at least pay me severance."

"Aguirre, I told you my hands were tied. Take this letter of recommendation and don't cause a scene."

Tears overflowed from Carolina's eyes, but anger and helplessness kept them at bay. She wouldn't allow herself to cry there, let alone "cause a scene."

As she descended the stairs, she cursed under her breath for taking that letter. But mostly for tearing it to shreds and tossing it into the air while shouting that she wouldn't sell herself out for a measly position. She tried to convince herself that it didn't count as a scene, but as a graceful exit.

❊ ❊ ❊

The empty cup only reminded her of the state of her life, without a job, partner, or plan for the future. Everything that days ago seemed like the start of an exciting journalism career was now a pile of bad decisions that started when she chose her major. Why couldn't she have studied Law like her mother wanted?

For the next half hour, Carolina imagined what Dr. Aguirre's life would be like while avoiding the gaze of the waiter who clearly wanted to collect payment for the coffee and clean the table she occupied. Her phone rang once more. The problem with being surrounded by people who make a living spreading news is that it becomes very difficult to keep a secret. Her close friends started calling her as soon as she left the newsroom: she had the urge to answer one of them and sent the others to voicemail. Minutes after her espresso arrived, her mother's calls began. It was the fifth time she hadn't answered, and she knew she was pushing her luck.

"The next time, I'll answer," she told herself, requesting the check.

She let it ring twice before picking up.

"Mom, I was on the street and didn't hear...," she began, but a cough interrupted her improvised excuse.

"Ms. Aguirre, I'm calling on behalf of Mr. Motta."

"Mariño, right?" she replied, sitting up. "Pitito didn't have the guts to call and apologize himself?"

"That's not why I'm calling," Mariño said quickly.

"I don't know what Pitito could want..."

"Mr. Motta," Mariño interrupted again. "Mr. Motta's campaign is reaching a critical point, and we can't afford any more... setbacks."

She wanted to retort, but Mariño's voice blocked her

attempt.

"Neither Mr. Motta nor his associates have the time to worry about trivial matters or baseless rumors that would only serve to... confuse public opinion. Do we understand each other?"

"I don't think, after what you did..."

"Ms. Aguirre, no one wants to do something they might... regret."

Carolina clenched her fist and took a deep breath before responding.

"Look, after what they did to me, the least..."

"This isn't a game; there are consequences."

The large stone shattered the window and struck the empty cup. The rock bounced twice more before hitting one of the beer coolers. Carolina's mind took a moment to catch up with what was happening. She locked eyes with the horrified faces of the other customers and only then noticed the shard of glass embedded in her forearm when the waiter approached to check on her.

"If you keep moving, I can't treat you," the paramedic said for the third time as she tried to stitch the wound. Carolina, agitated, scanned the room for any unfamiliar faces. They had checked her pulse and recommended she go to the hospital for further tests, but she had flatly refused. She couldn't shake the feeling that she was being followed and hadn't realized it.

Her phone vibrated. Carolina jumped, causing the doctor to start over. She took a deep breath before reaching for the phone, assuming it was her mother once again. However, the screen displayed a message from Mariño: "I hope we've come to an understanding."

Carolina turned off her phone with a sharp tap.

X

It took him a while to realize where he was. The sound of axes, followed by shouts, bangs, and curses, had woken him. He groped the concrete wall, his hand sliding off. It wasn't until he felt the fabric separating him from the outside that he remembered he was no longer behind bars. Stepping out of the tent, the scent of damp earth hit him, reminding him of the comforting feeling of digging his fingers into the sand the day before. A few meters away, Lechón wrestled with some wet branches and useless matches, greeting him with a smile.

"Want a mate?" A pale hand offered him one. "The others went down to the beach."

Maca got up earlier than the rest every day and prepared the mate. The hours and activities varied, but the mate round continued steadily until lunch.

Although the getaway to Santa Teresa had been good for everyone, Maca seemed to benefit the most: his constant smile and outstretched arm with a steaming mate became the most repeated image of the camp.

"The argument about how to light a fire with wet wood was intense," added Lechón as he blew on the feeble flames hiding among the branches.

"It was the best way to calm the mood," Maca chimed in.

"Differing approaches to the same problem," concluded Lechón before fully committing to his assigned task.

The Astute knew well how these small discussions about mundane problems could escalate. Scraping rice off the pot could lead to chemical and physical theories about the properties of metal, heat, and the history of crops in Uruguay. For once, he was grateful to have slept in and enjoyed two mates before starting a leisurely descent to the beach.

Upon arrival, he buried his feet in the still-cool sand and looked around. The beach was empty except for the dozen comrades gathered to celebrate many things, but mostly, the ability to do what they wanted. "Humans are creatures of habit," they told him multiple times when he mentioned that months after leaving prison, he still maintained the same routine. But there, hundreds of kilometers from his apartment, the sagging mattress, and the boring job, those daily rituals made no sense.

Sitting at the beach entrance, a few meters apart from the others, he let his toes play with the sand, savoring a morning he knew would be unique. Ahead of him, a casual soccer game was starting, and from the shouts, it seemed to be a rematch postponed since their time in the Penitentiary. To his right, a group shared a mate, while a few brave souls dared to try the water, challenging everyone to join them for a swim. El Ruso had already beaten them to it, barely visible in the distance with his long strokes. The Astute didn't approach anyone; he didn't need anything more. His joy came from seeing his comrades smile more than they had in decades.

He lay back on the sand, closed his eyes, and let the sounds of the sea and his friends lull him. He heard laughter, arguments, goal celebrations, songs, but he sat up when he heard a cry of pain.

"You're an animal! Damn it!" Pitito, clutching his leg, spat out sand angrily.

Two comrades helped him up, and it was clear he wouldn't be able to continue playing.

"Astute, stop sleeping and come here, we're one short!" they shouted from the makeshift field.

The Astute had no desire to move, much less run after a ball. However, this was one of those times when the needs of many outweighed the needs of one. He wasn't going to let them stop the game because of him.

"I'm in! Who am I playing with?"

Benteveo and Raquel emerged from the bushes behind the dunes. They walked a short distance from each other, trying to hide what everyone knew. The comrades had impeccable discipline for handling secrets, plans, and orders from superiors, but terrible self-control when it came to gossip. They had started seeing each other after a funeral, or a wedding, that part was unclear. But by the time Benteveo, after several whiskeys, decided to share the news with his close circle, everyone already knew.

Benteveo tossed his yellow shirt into the sand, and his prominent belly didn't prevent him from standing out among the kicks and shots.

❊ ❊ ❊

Off-season, the crackling of the huge bonfire of the group of ex-guerrillas was the only sound for several kilometers around. The night had moved past Lechón's exaggerated barbecue and the usual songs; and although the wine was still circulating, the mood had plummeted. The fun moments and happy memories brought up others that weren't so pleasant, the kind that tend to linger uninvited. What followed were lost gazes, sighs, and the obligatory passing of the jug of wine. A silent catharsis.

"Why don't we sing one more before we fall asleep? Who's got the guitar?" Maca stood up to get a better look.

"Why don't you shut up?" Benteveo interrupted him. "Consider yourself lucky we even let you come."

Eyes darted from one side to the other, there were approving smiles at Benteveo's remark, a few muttered comments, and two or three attempts to avoid an irreversible escalation.

"Bente, this isn't the time..." Pitito timidly added.

"Who says it isn't? If he had the audacity to come here, he should face the consequences," El Ruso quickly interjected, his voice rising to support the aggressive stance.

One or two comrades preferred to stand up and silently walk towards the tents. The rest watched

Maca, waiting for his next move. Most believed him guilty, many beyond any doubt, but they wanted to see him sweat and attempt to defend himself.

"Aren't you going to say anything, traitor?" Benteveo, heated by the alcohol, stood up from the makeshift bench. "You don't have the soldiers here to defend you."

Across the flames, Maca traced circles on the mouth of the jug, his eyes fixed on the ground.

"What's wrong, coward? What did you think would happen if you came camping with us? Did you think we'd forget?" El Ruso waved his massive arms as he crossed the bonfire towards the accused. Maca stepped back and fell on his back. Benteveo, Raquel, and El Ruso pounced on him, lifting him up in one swift motion and pinning him against the blazing bonfire. Pitito took several steps back, trying to distance himself from the scene and what might happen next. Several comrades tried to intervene, but were stopped halfway. The Russian wall wouldn't let them through.

The Astute hesitated; the resentment had clenched his fists so tightly that his nails dug into his palms, but he knew that if things got out of hand, there would be no stopping El Ruso and Benteveo together.

Maca's shirt was perilously close to being engulfed by the flames, yet he stood resolute and silent.

"Ruso..." the Astute cautiously placed a hand on his shoulder.

"Stay out of this! I want to know what he was offered to betray us. I want to see him on his knees," El Ruso threatened, turning towards the Astute and jabbing a finger into his chest.

"Let it go, this is getting out of hand," the Astute urged.

"If you want to go to sleep, go ahead," El Ruso insisted. "I want an explanation from this traitor."

"I want to know what happened too. But not like this," the Astute stepped forward, nudging Benteveo aside, and firmly grabbed Maca. "Come on, tell everything, or I'm heading to the tent and leaving you with them."

Maca moved away from the heat of the fire and took a long swig of wine. The small group surrounding him consisted of people who believed him a traitor and curious onlookers who had heard the story and now wanted to see how it would end. But they all anticipated a confession; the question was how forgiving the comrades, who had spent years in prison because of him, would be.

"I didn't do anything!" Maca suddenly shouted, waving the jug and approaching his accusers. "I didn't do anything! I'm not a snitch, damn it!"

"We saw you, Maca," El Ruso replied, now much calmer.

"I took a bullet! I was bleeding, and they threw me in the patrol car!" Maca lifted his tattered shirt and pointed to a spot below his ribs. No one could be sure what they were seeing. Was it a scar, a shadow, or soot from the firewood?

"Guys, let's calm down a bit," came a voice from the back.

"I won't calm down! I've been silently enduring this for years!" Maca continued to scream, his voice raw with emotion.

The shouting continued for a while longer, and gradually the comrades left the bonfire until only Maca remained, clutching the jug. The next day, several packed up and left, and the atmosphere never returned to normal; the sidelong glances and hushed accusations seemed ever-present. But despite everything, Maca stayed until the end, his head held high, whether out of innocence or stubbornness.

XI

The sound of her heels echoed on the asphalt. The wind blew fiercely, and the temperature had dropped at least fifteen degrees since early afternoon. Carolina walked hunched over, wrapped in a thin cardigan, looking down to conserve warmth. The five blocks between her apartment and the bus stop were usually an enjoyable walk after a long day at work. However, the wind, the cold, and the deserted, dark streets offered no such pleasure tonight. The only consolation was the thought of a pair of slippers waiting for her at home.

She jumped over a small puddle and saw a shadow move to her left. She stopped and observed more carefully. She heard a noise a few meters away, in front of an empty house, but couldn't distinguish anything unusual among the tall grass and neglected bushes. She had an urge to investigate and dispel her doubts about what was moving there, but decided to keep walking.

Something hit a 'FOR RENT' sign hanging in front of an old house. Her heels picked up the pace. She crossed the street against the light and walked faster. Were they following her? Was she in danger? Her pulse quickened, and her nerves grew with each step. Carolina tried to rationalize her behavior. There was no reason to be scared; she was acting like an idiot. Mariño's call was just that, a call. She had nothing to worry about.

Less than a block remained to reach the corner. She clutched her chest and tried to calm down. To her right, from the darkness of the street, a shadow rushed towards her. Her heart stopped. Carolina couldn't react, and a man in a suit and tie on a bicycle passed by and disappeared from sight.

She sighed, felt for her keys in her pocket, and walked the remaining meters as quickly as her shoes allowed. She reached the entrance of her building, climbed the steps to the door, and stopped to unlock it. A heavy hand landed on her shoulder. Carolina screamed, turned, and pressed herself against the entrance's glass.

"Carolina, did I scare you?"

To her eyes, the Astute looked like he had stepped

out of a horror movie. The worn black coat, the beard, and the tangle of hair would have frightened her even in daylight.

* * *

On paper, the tea should have calmed her; however, the fingers holding the cup wouldn't stop trembling. Carolina was pale, scared, and relieved at the same time. The Astute, sitting in one of the designer chairs in the small but stylish living room, watched her impassively. At first, he found her fright amusing, but after hearing about the call and the rock, he felt a familiar knot in his stomach. It had been years since he'd experienced that feeling.

"Can you figure out what they wanted with the computer?" the Astute asked, trying to distract her.

"I... I don't know... luckily El Ruso didn't have much installed," Carolina's fingers moved like a rehearsed choreography over the laptop's touchpad. To the Astute, it all seemed like magic. The screen changed colors, windows opened and closed under her attentive gaze and his amazement. Technology had surpassed him years ago. "Get friendly with it," Benteveo had often insisted, "You wouldn't believe what you can do with this. You can't imagine how I pick up women with my phone; they're all there." But the Astute knew when to admit defeat. That moment came during a "Computers and Internet for

Seniors" class when he assumed the CD drive was a coaster.

"I'm checking the most recently created and downloaded files..." she commented without taking her eyes off the screen. The Astute nodded as if he understood. "They seem to be... audio files... let's see..."

After a click, a familiar voice squeezed the Astute's heart. El Ruso cleared his throat and began the interview like a seasoned journalist, then shifted to a colloquial tone to greet the comrade in front of him.

"They're the interviews for the book," Carolina exclaimed. The Astute was still processing the sound of his friend's voice, only seeing her hands and lips move frenetically. She grabbed his shoulder and brought him closer to the screen. "One file is missing. An interview. That's what they deleted!"

The Astute struggled to understand what had happened.

"They killed him for the damn book?" he exclaimed incredulously. "It can't be..."

The Astute, hunched over with his hands on his face, appeared to sob quietly. Carolina said nothing. What could she say to comfort him when her recent experiences showed that what happened to El Ruso wasn't an isolated incident? After a while, the now much older ex-guerrilla, his eyes red from tears, returned to the computer screen.

"Can we find out which interview was deleted? Can it be recovered?"

She hesitated for a moment. It wasn't that she didn't know the answer—she had dealt with the problem of trying to recover a "mistakenly" deleted file several times—but she wasn't sure she wanted to go down that path, especially after the afternoon's incident. Was she so eager to tempt fate? Or did she really want to get a brick to the head?

"No... I don't think so..." she muttered, staring blankly.

But if she was so scared by a rock and a few threats, why had she wasted so many years studying and waiting for an opportunity like this? Why hadn't she taken that job as a weather reporter right out of college?

"Well... I have a friend who can look at it," Carolina said, sounding unconvinced. "But don't get your hopes up."

The Astute held his head in his hands. Now he wanted to know what had happened to El Ruso.

"Thanks for everything," he said, grabbing his coat. "Sorry for the trouble."

"Wait... what about the phone?"

"My phone? I think it's in my pocket," the Astute patted himself nervously.

"El Ruso's phone. Might it still have the recordings?"

"He didn't use it for that; he had just learned how to use WhatsApp," the tall man looked up at the ceiling as if chasing an elusive memory. "He always used that small recorder we gave him."

The excitement Carolina felt reminded her why she had chosen this profession.

XII

The murder had barely made a blip on that day's crime reports. A high-profile kidnapping and a case of domestic violence had hogged all the attention of the Montevidean press. The body was discovered in a ditch on the outskirts of a peripheral neighborhood; the victim had been shot, and authorities quickly chalked it up to a robbery gone wrong. Just another statistic. A man in his fifties, returning home from work, falling prey to the escalating violence plaguing the city streets.

Away from the media glare, the investigation continued. Forensics unearthed binding marks on the victim's wrists, indicating a calculated execution. A settling of scores. The remote location of the corpse suggested an attempt to cover up the crime. None of these details made it into the headlines. The visit of a Hollywood star to the country for a film shoot and the national soccer team's latest defeat dominated public discourse that week. Only one digital news outlet provided updates on the case, but it wasn't until the term "ex-Tupamaro" surfaced that the server crashed, thrusting the incident into the limelight. Unfortunately, it was at this moment that many of his former comrades learned of Maca's demise.

In the ensuing days, everyone had something to say about the death of the unknown guerrilla who eked out a living running a kiosk. Morning talk shows and YouTube channels dissected the murder du jour, yet the political leaders' responses sounded detached and perfunctory.

"If they couldn't remember him, they could at least have pretended," the Astute drained his glass of grappa as El Ruso flagged down the waiter.

"We'll need another round over here."

The waiter, seizing the opportunity to mop the floor while waiting for the last table to clear out, simply nodded resignedly.

"Perhaps it's better they keep quiet about him. I've had my fill of hearing about it," Benteveo's expression suddenly turned somber.

"Benteveo's got a point, Astute. Let it go. Who knows what he was involved in now."

The three of them continued to watch the old television hanging above the bar in silence. They knew that whatever they said would open old wounds and start an argument, and they hardly saw each other enough to end the night shouting.

"Hey, wasn't Pitito supposed to come?" El Ruso asked, breaking the silence.

The Astute shrugged, and both looked at Benteveo.

"How should I know? I'm not his dad," Benteveo finally said. "But I think he doesn't want to be seen with us. Political career and all."

"Here you go," the waiter's chubby fingers placed three glasses of grappa on the table. "Do you mind if I start closing out? I need to balance the register."

* * *

The night and that last drink seemed to have settled the matter of Maca for good. The next day, the journalists' interest shifted to a new criminal trend of blowing up ATMs with a gas cylinder and a car battery. Slowly, the news was filled with simulated explosions, videos of twisted ATMs, and explanations of why it was so easy to build that homemade explosive device. It was one of those mornings, as the Astute enjoyed the solitude while listening to the radio in the kitchen, that the murder of his former comrade once again became the focus. But this time, it would be very difficult for politicians and party activists to downplay its significance.

The announcement was brief. An anonymously sent photocopied letter had reached most of the capital's media outlets, signed by the R.G., the Reparation Group. The objective, highlighted in bold, was to seek justice and settle the blood debts from the guerrilla days. The letter concluded with concrete details: "Daniel Ernesto Macadar, known as El Maca, on August 12, 1969, was the one who shot and killed Sergeant Lionel Gutiérrez during the takeover of Banco la Caja Obrera."

"Did Maca kill him? Wasn't it...? But I clearly remember the shot, how could it be?" The Astute's bony fingers rubbed against his reddened eyes. "No. In '69, I was inside, I didn't participate." The Astute held his head. The pain had started abruptly, and he headed to the bathroom with his eyes closed, searching for a painkiller. It was common for this to happen, but that didn't make it any less painful. He swallowed the pills with some mate and lay down, waiting for the migraine to pass so he could once again distinguish between memories and the vivid accounts of his comrades.

XIII

A sudden pain shot through his back. The Astute doubled over, grabbing the railing of the staircase. He panted, clenched his teeth, and felt around his lower back, searching for the source. "Damn it! I survived the whole guerrilla war without getting shot, only to be taken down like this." He felt foolish for being so careless. What was he thinking? He had spent years training for situations like this, yet now he could barely breathe from the pain.

"Let me handle it," Benteveo's thick arms lifted the crate of books. "At your age, you should know better. You need to lift with your legs," he said, patting one of his quadriceps.

Embarrassed, the Astute leaned against the wall, hiding his pain until the truck left. Getting rid of so many things had been the hardest part—not because of sentimental value, but because it was difficult to find someone who wanted to take the amount of junk accumulated in that small apartment. Luckily, Carolina had found a bookseller willing to buy El Ruso's eclectic collection of books. One problem and several boxes fewer to worry about.

Benteveo entered the semi-empty apartment and extended his hand.

"You didn't have to come," the Astute said, standing up with signs of pain. "I could have managed... even if it would have taken a bit longer..."

"You'd have ended up in the hospital, old man! Besides, doesn't the truck charge you by the hour? Be thankful my swimming class got canceled, and I came to help you out."

"Yeah, well..." The Astute dusted off his pants and started rummaging through the boxes still occupying the kitchen corners. "I didn't remember telling you the date."

"But you booked it with me. Is this trash?" Benteveo asked, seconds away from dumping his mate over a bag of papers and broken plastics.

"Wait, let me see..." The Astute carefully examined each crumpled paper as if it might hide a treasure. Benteveo watched him incredulously.

"Forget it, I'll dump the yerba at home."

Crack! The sound of plastic breaking came from the kitchen, followed by timid footsteps on the tiled floor of the living room. The Astute turned his head, listening with his better ear, while Benteveo pulled a revolver from his waistband and rushed toward the apartment entrance.

"That guy won't get away again."

The Astute couldn't react. The gunshot startled him, and the woman's scream churned his insides with a terror he hadn't felt in years. When he reached the living room, Carolina was on her knees, crying from the nerves, and Benteveo, slumped in the only remaining chair, was breathing heavily. The gun was still smoking.

"I swear, I thought it was the guy who broke in last time," Benteveo said, holding his head.

The bullet had chipped the plaster just a meter from the girl, the only witness to the narrowly avoided tragedy, thanks to the declining aim of a man nearing seventy. Carolina, either impassive or in shock, took off her shoes and cleaned the plastic shards from her heel.

"Sorry, I broke the CD case," she said, picking up

the remnants of volume one of Harry Belafonte's All Time Greatest Hits and handing it to the Astute, as if nothing else had happened.

"Don't worry, El Ruso was the only one who enjoyed Belafonte."

"Coconut Woman" played at a volume too low to bother the neighbors or anyone present. Everyone had been surprised to find that the old CD player, collecting dust on the TV, still worked. "You could get a few bucks for this," Benteveo had said. "Or better yet, you could replace that crappy radio."

"What are you doing here?" the Astute asked, trying to steady his nerves.

"You said you were coming. Don't you remember?" She put on one shoe again and inspected the sole of the other. "Did you find the recorder?"

The Astute shook his head.

"We searched everywhere," Benteveo chimed in. "This scavenger even went through the trash multiple times. You know, a new one isn't that expensive," he said, rubbing his elbow and giving Carolina a knowing look.

"You nearly scared us to death," the Astute, still nervous, clutched his tea cup as if it were slippery with soap.

"Let's not talk about who could have killed whom," Carolina used her shoe to point at the hole in the wall.

The Astute looked down, and Benteveo muttered under his breath. The tense silence was only broken by Harry Belafonte and the Astute's sips of tea until Benteveo cracked his back as he stood up.

"Well, I better get going if I want to make it to my tai chi class."

"Pitito called me last night," Carolina blurted out suddenly.

Benteveo sat back down.

"What did he want?" The Astute straightened up and set his cup aside. "What did he say?"

"Nothing. He wanted to give me an interview," she looked up, trying to recall the conversation precisely. "He said it was serious... and that he had an exclusive. I don't know. It was all very strange."

"Why strange?" Benteveo, who seemed to have forgotten about tai chi, reached out and turned off the CD player with a flick.

"He was nervous, talking very fast, and I could hear someone yelling in the background. I think it was Mariño," she adjusted her shoe and stood up. "He was angry and telling him to hang up."

"What are you going to do?"

"What can I do? I scheduled the interview for tomorrow morning."

Carolina dusted off her skirt and walked to the door. But before leaving, she turned, wagging her index finger in the air as if she had remembered something important that the near-death experience had made her forget.

"Locked in here, you might not be aware, but the R.G. claimed responsibility for El Ruso's murder," Carolina showed them her phone screen from a distance, where one of the news portals echoed the Ministry of Interior's announcement. Neither Benteveo nor the Astute could see anything from that distance, but they said nothing. "The letters arrived this morning."

Carolina left the apartment. The Astute and Benteveo remained in silence.

XIV

The bullet whistled over the Astute's head. He crouched behind the white Fusca, making sure his entire body was shielded by the car. Another bullet hit the window, shattering the glass of the passenger door. Amidst the cacophony, screams echoed, but it was impossible to tell where they were coming from.

A lifeless body lay a few meters away. Blood soaked the sidewalk, staining the bananas at the vegetable stand. A bit farther, in the street and exposed, lay the Astute's revolver.

"Did you drop it?! You've got to be kidding me! Duck your head, don't lose it too!" Benteveo charged at the soldiers, firing and searching for cover. It was like watching Hopalong Cassidy in one of his movies, and the Astute smiled briefly at the resemblance. However, now, ten minutes later, with no sign of Benteveo or any other comrades, nothing seemed funny anymore. Anxiety became unbearable, and he increasingly considered raising his hands and surrendering, knowing full well that it could mean a bullet in the chest or, worse, weeks of torture.

What else could he do? It was clear that the robbery hadn't gone according to plan, and they hadn't anticipated any contingency measures for the current scenario. There were no procedures for "dropping the weapon while crossing the street," he thought, and surrendering didn't seem as bad as having to listen to Benteveo recounting this disaster over and over again.

The siren drowned out the shouts and gunfire. A green truck parked urgently. Nearly a dozen soldiers got out, firing in all directions. The Astute grabbed his head and knew he was lost. Suddenly, the shots on the Volkswagen protecting him ceased. The ammunition from all the weapons was directed to the opposite sidewalk. The Astute, still covering his head, turned to see what was happening. Raquel, gritting her teeth and carrying a submachine gun, leaped over the hood of a truck and ran into the street, unleashing a burst of gunfire at the soldiers. Screams and calls for help rang out. The police cordon seemed to be in chaos as the officers tried to get the wounded out of the line of fire. Raquel leaped again, appearing beside the Astute and leaning against the Fusca's chassis. The SA25 submachine gun smelled of burnt gunpowder. Of course, the

Astute had no idea what weapon it was; it was only years later that he learned the name, hearing the feat recounted countless times by other comrades.

"Shall we?" she said as she replaced the magazine.

The Astute didn't manage to nod before Raquel took his hand and, after unleashing a savage hail of bullets toward the exposed soldiers, pulled him to the truck waiting on the corner.

* * *

It was nine in the morning on a rainy Sunday in Montevideo. One of those days when the already sad gray facades of the city's buildings seemed even sadder and grayer. On the table sat a half-eaten mozzarella, a warm cheese sandwich, a liter bottle of beer, two glasses, and a coffee.

"Isn't it a bit early for a drink, Benteveo?" The Astute tried to mask his concern.

"Leave him alone," El Ruso said, still chewing on his mozzarella. "Meal times are imperialist impositions."

Without swallowing, El Ruso lifted the bottle and poured beer for Benteveo. The glass overflowed with foam, wetting the paper napkin that served as a makeshift tablecloth. Nothing in all their years of guerrilla warfare, torture, and imprisonment had prepared them for this. How did one deal with the constant wakes of comrades? How did one endure social protocol when so many had departed prematurely? But above all, what did one do in situations like this? None of the three knew. They ate and drank in silence, the weight of the past few hours heavy on their shoulders and eyelids.

They had arrived at the funeral home late at night, and the place resembled a supermarket on Christmas Eve. Live broadcasts from local channels, photographers, and journalists lurked in every corner. Politicians, public figures, "celebrities," nobodies, and gawkers. Even Raquel's family, who had shunned her since the guerrilla days, was now among the mourners. Being a Tupamaro was trendy. And for the older ones, the circus surrounding the President had very little to do with what they had experienced.

They found Raquel on Saturday morning hanging from a tree in front of her house. The coroner's report stated that despite the beatings she had received, the cause of death was the two gunshot wounds to her head and chest. The printed statement from the Reparation Group was hidden in one of her pockets. It came as no surprise to anyone that she was the group's second victim: Raquel's bloody exploits, as well as her involvement in robberies, kidnappings, and the escapes from

Punta Carretas prison and Cabildo prison, had been well-documented in chronicles and books. In fact, outside of the leadership and famous party figures, she was the most obvious target. So much so that after Maca's death, some of her comrades offered her help to hide or emigrate. She gave them all the same answer: "Let them come find me one by one."

"You know..." Benteveo emptied his beer glass in one gulp and slammed it on the table. "Raquel caused a hell of a fuss when you didn't come out of prison," he addressed the Astute, but his gaze was fixed on the tiled floor.

El Ruso hurried to refill his glass and poured some for himself as well. The Astute's fingers played with a teaspoon. He didn't say anything. Benteveo would continue the story if he wanted and when he was ready.

"When Lechón told her you weren't going up the tunnel..." Benteveo continued. "She went after Pepe, Pepe! Can you believe it? She was a wild one..." He downed his glass once more. "But damn, she could fuck."

El Ruso nodded in approval and ordered another beer.

"And won't you bring me a tea with lemon and honey?" Pitito left a stack of newspapers on the table and pulled out a chair to sit. The others looked at him in amazement. "What? My throat," he said, gesturing to his Adam's apple. "I've got a speaking engagement. Need to keep my voice in shape."

Pitito sat down and placed his hand on Benteveo's shoulder.

"How are you?"

"Fine," Benteveo replied, pulling his shoulder away and grabbing another slice of mozzarella.

"Relax, the leadership promised me this won't go unanswered," Pitito insisted. "They're already digging into it."

No one responded. None of them wanted to revisit the murder. It wasn't the right time, and the oppressive silence, only interrupted by El Ruso's chewing, was finally broken when the waiter approached the table.

"Can you move the newspapers so I can leave this?" The Astute noticed the teacup trembling in the waiter's hand. Pitito quickly made space on the table, and the Astute took the opportunity to glance at one of the newspapers.

"Page twelve," Pitito said, pushing the others aside.

The waiter, somewhat annoyed, left the honey and the teacup, took the empty beer bottle, and set down a full one.

"Have you seen this?" The Astute gripped the newspaper, fuming. "Did you read what they wrote about Raquel? Unbelievable!"

Benteveo lowered his head, and El Ruso leaned over to read over the Astute's shoulder.

"What bastards! Who wrote this crap?"

"It doesn't matter," Pitito replied, carefully sipping his tea to avoid burning himself. "They're all the same. The press will end up killing us if we don't do something."

XV

The open casket had been an express request from the campaign manager; however, the expression on Pitito's face was just another cruel twist of fate. He seemed to be smiling at everyone who came to pay their respects, as if refusing to accept the situation. During the few hours of the wake, comments about the grin on his face overshadowed the fact that an up-and-coming politician had been murdered, and the police were already interrogating a suspect.

The Astute found out by turning on the radio and, trembling, called Benteveo, who was still sleeping. Neither of them wanted to go to the wake alone. The pain of losing yet another friend weighed heavily on their chests, but the main reason was that they didn't want to face the hypocrisy of the political class and the empty, formal greetings. To get to the wake, they had to pass a block of journalists and photographers and be frisked at the entrance. This was the first sign of growing paranoia about another possible assassination by the Reparation Group. Sporadic in the past, the attacks had now happened within a few days, and the authorities had two dead Tupamaros, one of whom was a candidate for senator in the upcoming—and very near—elections.

As soon as he crossed the threshold of the funeral parlor, the Astute lost track of Benteveo. Initially, he thought Benteveo might have gone to the bathroom, but minutes later, he imagined him clutching a glass of wine and reminiscing with party comrades. The Astute began walking towards the small dimly lit room where the casket awaited, knowing he didn't want to see the body but could distract himself by "admiring" the floral arrangements to make the torturous obligatory minutes pass quickly.

Engulfed in a thick fog of handshakes, kisses, hugs, condolences, and furtive glances, the Astute seemed to wander aimlessly through the room. Several people who approached him were complete strangers; however, it was he who sparked the most curiosity among those present. Who was this disheveled-looking man, even by the party's standards? It wasn't until Mujica greeted him with an enthusiastic hug that people stopped scrutinizing him so closely.

Suddenly, a large man in a suit asked the attendees

to make way and clear the entrance. The Astute was pushed against a table laden with sandwiches and had to contort himself to avoid getting butter on his pants. The doors of the room swung open, and a crowd of supporters clad in the party's colors burst in. They marched with flags and banners held high until they reached the room with the casket. The anticlimactic end to their entrance came when they had to enter in groups of five to say goodbye to Pitito, who seemed to find the situation quite amusing.

He was halfway through a ham and cheese sandwich when he saw the cursive letters. From that distance, he could even make out the phrase they formed: "crazy about you" and what appeared to be the Peñarol crest.

"Murderer!" he yelled, tossing the sandwich aside.

The young man spun around, saw the Astute pushing through the crowd, dropped the flag, and bolted. The mob turned into a tumult, and no one understood what was happening, although several, catching sight of the Astute, confirmed their suspicions that he had come to steal.

The narrow hallway with its worn carpet led to a meeting room, likely used for receiving important clients. The Astute leaped over a fallen chair and continued toward the open door on the other side of the room. He was greeted by a somber hall with coffins on display. The young man was at the far end and ran toward what appeared to be an exit onto the street. The Astute's effort was futile; he knew he couldn't keep up with, let alone catch him. Out on the street, the young man picked up speed, and the Astute had to stop to catch his breath. Several meters ahead and disappearing into the crowd, the young man seemed to have gotten away. The Astute couldn't continue, but he wasn't about to let himself be defeated again. He shouldered his way past a middle-aged couple strolling with mate and snatched their thermos.

The clang of the young man hitting the metal pole echoed from across the street. The thermos had struck his calves. After stumbling and staggering into a street stall selling cellphone protectors, the young man collapsed against a "Yield" sign.

"Why did you kill him?!" the Astute, furious, shook the young man by the shirt. "Tell me why, you bastard!"

Still groggy, the young man mumbled nonsensical words and struggled to wave him off.

"Leave him. He didn't do anything. I sent him to El Ruso's house."

The Astute's knuckles pounded repeatedly into that smug face. His labored breathing didn't stop him, nor did the shouts he felt all around him.

"I'm going to kill you! You bastard!"

XVI

The sun was setting when they finally let him out of the station. "He's not pressing charges," they told him. "Why does it matter?" insisted the officer who seemed to have been stuck behind a desk for hours. "Go celebrate, you got lucky this time."

Stepping out of the precinct, the darkness threw him off. He didn't remember spending that many hours inside, and his internal clock no longer worked like it used to. He rubbed his eyes to shake off the disorientation and, with blurred vision, noticed someone approaching.

"What are you doing here?"

"I found Pitito dead," said Carolina, her hair disheveled and looking as exhausted as he felt, emerging from the same door.

"What?"

"Hold on, I need a beer—or several—before I explain," she said, slipping on her jacket and walking down the block.

* * *

"Sit him down... in that chair," Mariño's stubby fingers fished a bundle of zip ties out of the desk drawer.

Bruised and slightly dazed, the Astute still tried to resist, but the two hulking security guards forced him into the chair, securing his arms and legs.

"Are you going to kill me too?" he spat, masking his fear.

Mariño reached into his pocket, searching for his cell phone.

"So you're astute but not smart," he said, eyes fixed on the screen. "We're waiting for the police, and I don't want you running off again."

"Fine, let them come. They can hear everything," the Astute said, puffing out his chest.

With a subtle gesture, Pitito's campaign coordinator signaled the security guards to leave the room.

He sat behind the desk and sighed, searching for patience.

"Look, Astute..." It was strange hearing him speak so carefully. "I didn't do what you're thinking."

The veins in the Astute's arms looked like they were about to burst. "I saw it!" he hissed, his voice low and dangerous. "I saw that kid at El Ruso's house. What did you forget the day you went to kill him?"

Mariño, seemingly unbothered, stood up and retrieved a box of Chivas Regal 12 from a cabinet. "I'd heard that the imagination of the Tupamaros was... colorful, but I didn't think it went this far," he said, pouring himself a drink. "I was saving this for when we won, but now... what does it matter?"

The Astute's silent, pent-up fury seemed to make the chair he was tied to tremble. Mariño leaned against the table, facing him. "Look, I'll set things straight just because of the fondness Wilton had for you. Did you know he tried to convince me more than once to add you to the party's candidate list?"

The Astute's expression was unchanging. Mariño sighed softly. "Wilton gave an interview to Yanquelevich, for the book."

"To El Ruso?" The Astute shook his head. "But he was the one most opposed..."

Mariño shrugged. "After Raquel Acosta's death, his stance changed. Despite my advice, he gave the interview and said some things that could... compromise him politically. An idiot. He threw three years of campaigning in the trash," Mariño continued, downing the whiskey in one gulp. "When Yanquelevich was killed, we knew there was a chance the audio could go public, or worse, implicate Motta. That's why I had it erased."

Mariño contemplated the bottle while the Astute remained silent, processing what he'd heard.

"And that's why you killed Pitito," he finally concluded.

"I didn't kill anyone!" Mariño quickly regained his composure. "Why would I kill him two months before the election? I invested three years in this..."

Suddenly, the Astute lowered his voice, and his words became inaudible.

"What can I get you?" A girl with curly hair and a perpetual smile stopped at their table.

"Just a beer," the Astute replied.

"Alright," she said, typing on a tablet. "I can recommend a mango IPA, strong but with just the right bitterness."

"A what?"

"Do you prefer a stout? We have an oatmeal one..."

"Oatmeal?" The Astute adjusted himself in the chair. "I want a beer, not a smoothie." He glanced at Carolina, who was laughing heartily. "Where did you bring me?"

"A mild one, a golden ale for him," Carolina ordered to avoid further discomfort for the Astute. "And the mango IPA for me."

"Do you believe Mariño?" Carolina asked, taking long sips from her craft beer.

"As scummy as he is, it doesn't make sense that he killed them."

"And now?"

"We still have El Ruso's computer," the Astute cautiously sniffed his beer.

Carolina shook her head. "The file is irretrievable.

We won't know what Pitito said." She emptied her glass and held it up to order another. "In the end, my friend couldn't do anything."

"Then that's it."

"It can't be..." Carolina struggled to contain her frustration as the waitress approached with her drink.

"You know, that whole 'there is no perfect crime' thing is a lie, especially in our country," the Astute said, taking a sip of his beer and wiping the foam from the corner of his mouth. "But still, keep the interviews. Maybe they'll help you write something."

Carolina hadn't considered that. Her mind was consumed by El Ruso's murder. Not even the worry of how she would pay next month's rent seemed to distract her.

XVII

His stomach made noises he hadn't heard in months. By now, there were only a few bites left of the chorizo sandwich, but he wished there were many more. The Tupamaros locked up in Punta Carretas had "ways" of getting meat and the occasional luxury food item, but it was never enough for everyone and never tasted as good. Nothing seemed to diminish the pleasure, not even knowing that this luxury was meant to ease the guilt they felt for leaving him behind. While savoring the delicacy, he imagined himself sitting on a sidewalk in Palermo on a summer day, amidst wine and grilled meat at one of the many spontaneous street gatherings. Ever since Pepe told him he wouldn't be leaving with the others, that "it was important for the movement that he continued working from inside," everyone had been more attentive to him.

"Well? How is it?" Lechón had taken the news

very badly and was one of those most concerned with finding him something to quell his afternoon hunger.

The Astute couldn't answer. He closed his eyes and smiled with a grimace, still chewing.

All week, the attention and gifts continued, which were nothing more than food and smuggled tools, but no less special for it. The leadership invited him to share a meal with them, and he could swear Benteveo let him score a goal in their Thursday soccer game. The situation was difficult for him to handle. The Astute, responsible for welcoming and guiding newcomers, was used to being the one solving problems for his comrades. Now, he felt like a lifer who everyone felt a bit sorry for.

"Hey, are you gonna eat all that?" El Ruso's index finger pointed at the cheese and the jar of dulce de leche resting on the Astute's lap.

The Astute gripped what was left of his chorizo sandwich with one hand to protect the last gifts he had received with the other.

"You know you're the only one who comes asking instead of bringing me something?"

"I don't feel guilty. If it were up to me, you'd be out first, and the leadership would stay behind," El Ruso said, taking the jar and opening it with one hand.

Three knobby fingers dug into the dulce de leche and scooped out almost half of what was in the jar.

"You know next week you'll be able to eat whatever you want, right?" The Astute hurried to finish the last of his chorizo sandwich.

"Yeah, but it won't be the same," El Ruso replied, fingers still in his mouth. "Here, it has a special taste."

The Astute smiled quietly. Of all those allowed to escape, it was El Ruso he would miss the most. He was the only one who had protested the decision, even when the Astute acted as if staying in prison didn't matter. Three days ago, El Ruso confronted the leadership, trying to change their minds and nearly coming to blows. "Why are we leaving him when we have space for common prisoners?" he had challenged Ñato during recess in the yard. Without a word, two burly comrades grabbed him by the arms and escorted him to a cell on the ground floor. El Ruso's strength required another two Tupamaros to help contain him. Behind them, Benteveo and the Astute followed with concern. Even knowing that part of the guard had been bribed, the possibility of information leaking just days before the escape had everyone on edge. No one knew how the leadership might react; however, El Ruso's fury earned him only a reprimand. Most Tupamaros would go to great lengths to avoid a fight with him.

El Ruso's fingers were coated with dulce de leche again, and he pointed them at the Astute before putting them in his mouth.

"Have you seen Pitito yet?"

The Astute shook his head, and El Ruso scooped up more dulce before resuming the conversation.

"He was looking for you this afternoon. I told him you were working in the tunnel. I think he had some things for you."

"It must be the stout he was brewing last week!" Pitito's specialty, made with eggs, coffee, and yeast, was highly coveted among the comrades. "I'll go get it before someone else drinks it. Can you keep an eye on him, Lechón?"

Lechón nodded, and the Astute closed the cell door behind him.

"Do you have a knife?" El Ruso asked, grabbing the cheese.

Pitito's cell was directly above the Astute's, but to get there, he had to walk a few meters to the stairs and then cross half a block. Along the way, he received a hammer, a scarf with a warning that the next winter would be "cruel," and three honey candies. He thanked everyone with the same polite smile, eager to escape the discomfort of being one of the few left behind in the prison. Hurrying into Pitito's cell, he didn't expect to find what he did.

"Sorry... I didn't know."

The Astute woke with a start.

XVIII

"...it's a rap I wrote myself," the young man declared, placing the enormous boombox on an empty seat and turning on the music.

Over the cacophony that filled the bus, the Astute tried to focus on what he would say when he arrived, but the lack of rhythm and nonsensical rhymes made it impossible to concentrate. However, the anxiety and trembling in his hands had lessened thanks to the music—so he tossed some coins into the baseball cap.

Since waking from his nap, he'd been in a fog that made it hard to think clearly. He left his apartment without even having a mate or turning on the radio. His phone rang while he was in the elevator, but the Astute didn't pay attention, as if he couldn't comprehend where the sound was coming from. Once outside, he wandered aimlessly, his eyes half-closed, muttering under his breath. Like an overloaded processor, his movements were erratic, and it seemed like he could collapse at any moment. If he had been more lucid, he would have noticed the comments from the people he passed and a woman pulling her child out of his path. After a few blocks of aimless wandering, he made a determined beeline for a bus stop and boarded. Those who saw him stagger and talk to himself hoped he got on the right bus; the Astute hoped the same.

When he got off, a familiar sensation washed over him, and for a moment, he forgot why he had come. Nothing snaps you back to reality like being a few steps from the front door: a slap of reality right before ringing the bell.

There was no answer. He rang three times and knocked on the door: same result. Determination turned to uncertainty, and suddenly, he didn't know what to do.

By the time he realized what he was trying to accomplish, he had already climbed the wall, with his left hand gripping a pipe to hoist himself into the inner courtyard. His knees screamed "crack" to announce to his body that they had landed. The Astute collapsed and took almost a minute to get up and walk toward the back. Through the windows, he saw no one inside. The living room was empty, and everything was off. He moved to the back and tried to force the kitchen door. No luck.

The idea of returning home empty-handed was becoming less appealing. He went to the shed in the back and opened the window with a trick he learned during his clandestine years. He was sure that a copy of the kitchen key was kept there for emergencies.

The only window was boarded up, and light only entered through small cracks in the wall, gaps left by missing roof tiles, and the dirty glass of a small skylight. In the twilight of the evening, the darkness of the shed revealed only silhouettes against the blackness. The Astute fumbled around and managed to turn on a flashlight.

The most promising piece of furniture was a battered dresser covered with several cans of paint. The top drawer was already open and held only some nuts and a rusty faucet. The second drawer contained a few bullet casings, a lock—without a key—and a ceramic ornament missing several pieces. "This is pointless," thought the Astute as he struggled to open the next drawer.

The third drawer came out entirely. Inside, next to a Walkman and a bunch of old batteries, he found a digital recorder. Could it be El Ruso's? How could he tell? He didn't even remember the brand, only that it was small and digital. Regardless, the memory was empty. The recorder proved nothing, but the Astute kept looking. An unopened pack of envelopes caught his attention. A few inches away, there was a small stack of printed pages face down. He took one and turned it over.

"Damn it!" The Astute furiously crumpled the paper. He checked the others; they were all the same: printed statements from the Reparation Group claiming responsibility for the murder of Pitito Motta. Stunned, he searched for something to lean on.

He needed to tell someone—the party leaders, the police. His trembling fingers gripped the cellphone. When the screen lit up, he saw a notification. He had a voicemail from Carolina.

"Astute, I finally took your advice and I'm going to use the interviews. But I want to do a few myself, to give it my own touch. Anyway... I'd like to interview you again, if you don't mind, of course. I can't today because I've already scheduled with Benteveo. Let me know when it's convenient for you. Cheers."

XIX

Logic dictated that she should have been more nervous; however, there were few mornings when she felt this calm. She had waffles and a latte for breakfast while gazing out the window, instead of gulping down three sips of black coffee while checking her phone. She had also decided to leave early and walk the twenty blocks from her apartment to Pitito's office. She should have been more nervous; that way, she might have noticed something was off.

"I didn't see anything," she repeated to the police when they questioned her at the station. It was true, she didn't possess any of the sharp senses journalists flaunted in the movies. She barely remembered what she was thinking when she got off the elevator, opened the office door, and found Pitito in a pool of blood.

With his pants and underwear down, Pitito lay on

the gray carpet in the reception area. His yellow shirt had a circular bloodstain that ended in a deep gunshot wound. Carolina stood frozen next to the corpse for a few minutes. She fought the urge to run without looking back, but kept reminding herself that doing so would only land her in bigger trouble. She crouched over the body and brought her ear close to Pitito's face, trying to detect any breath. Her shoe slipped in the blood, and Carolina fell onto the corpse. As she tried to get up without slipping again, her blood-soaked hands left animal print-like marks on Pitito's clothes.

She decided to call 911. Surely the forensic police could prove she wasn't a murderer, just a clumsy person with terrible luck. She looked at Pitito one last time, and despite her disdain for him, she could only feel compassion in that moment. She pulled up his pants and then dialed emergency services.

Almost eight days had passed, but every time she saw a gray surface, Pitito and the pool of blood appeared on it.

"Is it okay if I sit here?"

Benteveo and his prominent belly moving among the furniture in the tiny living room snapped her out of the trance.

"Yes, wherever you like. I'll bring the microphone

closer, don't worry."

Carolina took the two cups of coffee and placed them on the coffee table. She turned on the recorder and positioned the microphone towards Benteveo.

"Okay, tell me, how did you meet Pitito?" she asked as she opened a worn notebook.

"What does Pitito have to do with this? I thought we were going to talk about El Ruso."

Carolina leaned back and took a sip of coffee.

"It gives me a bit of context about how your relationships were."

"You're barking up the wrong tree, miss," Benteveo adjusted himself to stand up. "Look, I get that you found Pitito, and that affected you. If you want, I can come back in a few days."

Carolina felt offended by the dismissive tone and angry because she knew Benteveo was right. Finding Pitito's corpse had shaken her more than she had anticipated.

"What do you think? That I've never seen a dead body?" she lied, puffing out her chest. "I used to work at a newspaper; you wouldn't believe the things you see there."

Benteveo smirked, aware that Carolina was lying, but he admired her stoic demeanor in the face of unexpected situations.

"Okay, but seeing one like that, with all the blood and in such a compromising position," he finally replied.

"Compromising?"

"With his dick out."

It took Carolina a few seconds to react. She stepped back, clutching her chest, and rose from the couch. She walked toward the kitchen, assessing her options. From the living room, Benteveo watched her curiously. "The best thing is to act like nothing's wrong and speed up the interview," she told herself, her inner voice trembling.

"Uh... I'm going to add some milk to my coffee. Do you want any?" murmured Carolina without looking up.

"No, mine's fine."

She tried to keep an eye on him through the mirror but ended up spilling the milk on the counter.

"Damn it!"

"Are you okay? Need a hand?" Benteveo exclaimed, getting to his feet.

"No, no, I'm fine." Carolina slowly walked back to the living room and picked up her phone from the table. "But I think you were right, it's better if we leave this for another day."

Benteveo watched her silently for a few seconds. Carolina took a step back and unlocked her phone screen. It took him a moment to react, but he was already moving towards her when they were interrupted by loud knocks on the door.

"Carolina! Are you there? Carolina!" The Astute was pounding on the door vehemently.

Inside the apartment, neither of them moved a muscle; their gazes locked, each trying to predict the other's next move. The knocking intensified.

"Carolina!"

Benteveo took a step forward, and Carolina's phone began to ring.

"What are you going to do?" she challenged. "Kill me and then him too?

Carolina lifted her phone and showed the screen to Benteveo. The incoming call was from the Astute.

"Carolina, I hear the phone! Open up, it's important!" he shouted from outside, hammering the door with his fist again.

With the last blow, the door seemed to give way and swung open wide. From inside, Benteveo gestured roughly for him to come in. The Astute entered briskly, locking eyes with Carolina (still clutching her phone), and Benteveo slammed the door shut behind him.

XX

"Shhhuuic, shuuuic." The mate passed quickly between them in a two-person round as another thermos of water ran out. Afternoon had turned to night, and the empty bag of pastries on the table was the only evidence of their long conversation, along with their aching jaws from so much laughter.

"Should I heat more water, or is it time for something stronger?" El Ruso waved the thermos in the air to confirm it was empty.

"Do you even have to ask?" Benteveo leaned back, eyeing the cabinet in the library where he knew there was always an unopened bottle of grappa. "For emergencies," El Ruso would say when asked.

El Ruso brought down the bottle, pulled two glasses from a shelf, and blew the dust off before setting them on the table. Benteveo quickly made room by crumpling the bakery bag and moving the still-off recorder aside. Friendship and catching up came first.

"To friends who always stick around!" El Ruso solemnly raised his glass.

"To the code of honor. It's what holds us together in the end," Benteveo clinked his glass against El Ruso's.

At first glance, Benteveo and El Ruso were very similar: big, heavy drinkers, fans of the Bella Vista football team, and above all, hot-tempered. But that's where the similarities ended. El Ruso, except for his worn jeans that seemed glued to his legs, was neat, kept in shape, had short hair slicked back with pomade, and shaved religiously every morning. Across the table, Benteveo's belly bulged under a T-shirt full of pastry crumbs. His thick beard and unruly gray locks looked like they hadn't been combed in decades. But for those who spent months or years sharing hideouts or cells with them, the difference was in their eyes. El Ruso's gaze exuded confidence. Even in his worst rages, those facing him knew what to expect. Benteveo's eyes, however, were blank, evasive, and all his reactions were a surprise.

Since the red light on the recorder started blinking, Benteveo couldn't find a comfortable position on the couch. It was only thanks to the bottle of grappa that he managed to relax, so much so that every two questions, the interview roles would switch.

"And are you going to put all this in the book?" Benteveo asked as he brought the glasses closer to pour more.

"I don't know... it depends. All of this..." El Ruso lifted the recorder and held it in the air. "It's raw material, it's impossible to say right now."

"You're not going to put our stuff in, right?"

"There's nothing that isn't 'our stuff.'"

"I'm serious," Benteveo paused to down his glass in one gulp. "There are places better left unexamined. You should be careful."

El Ruso set the grappa down and stood up.

"Are you threatening me or warning me?"

Both men's muscles tensed.

"Depends on how stubborn you are..."

Mrs. García de Molina, who had lived on that block for nearly 45 years, told the police she was awakened by the first shot. However, it was her poodle's barking, not the noise, that got her out of bed. The second shot surprised her in the bathroom, just before flushing the toilet. She also omitted this in her police report.

Despite the rivers of blood pouring from his chest, El Ruso clung to life with the stubbornness worthy of a Tupamaro. His fingers gripped the armrests of the chair as if staying in contact with the physical world could prevent his organs from failing.

Standing in front of him, Benteveo surveyed the room, evaluating his next steps. El Ruso's wheezing breath and distant barks were all that could be heard. After cleaning any evidence that could place him there and pocketing the recorder, Benteveo sat down to finish the grappa.

"Ben... te," El Ruso managed to say, blood spilling from his mouth.

Benteveo looked up and drew his gun.

"...you son of a bitch," El Ruso whispered.

There was no need for a third shot.

"And you're a fucking snitch."

XXI

"I told you I don't care."

Raquel slipped on the red thong, the elastic snapping against her wide hips. For a woman over sixty, Raquel was still striking, drawing eyes wherever she went, even without makeup and with her hair untidy.

"Do you think I'm an idiot? You made a fool out of me!" Benteveo, lying naked on his back on the bed, pointed at her with a beer bottle that had gone warm in the midday heat.

"I wasn't mocking you. Don't be stubborn," Raquel tried to lower the tone of the argument.

"I know that little laugh," Benteveo sat up to take a swig.

"If I smiled, it's because I was surprised to see a... I

don't know... different side of you. That's all."

"Something different? What do you mean by that?" he said, walking towards her threateningly. "Are you calling me a sissy?"

On her knees, Raquel was looking for the rest of her clothes but looked up to answer.

"Please, Bente, let it go."

She reached out to grab her pants from under the bed and shook them out before putting them on. She zipped them up and took a deep breath.

"I don't care what you did in prison," she approached and stroked Benteveo's hairy forearm. "And if it helped you and Pitito get through that tough time, then I'm glad for both of you."

Benteveo was speechless. Normally, he would have responded in a way that escalated the argument to the point of blowing the roof off, but to Raquel's surprise, he retreated in silence. She considered going to hug him but chose instead to finish getting dressed.

"Have you seen my bra?"

Benteveo didn't answer, turning his back and lifting the bottle.

"I shouldn't have told you anything. You can't help yourself; you have to mock," he muttered to himself, aware that Raquel could hear him.

"Did you hear a word I said? Or am I talking to myself, as usual?" Half-naked, she stopped defiantly in front of him.

The bottle remained in the air, and Benteveo's Adam's apple bobbed up and down with the rhythm of the beer. Raquel huffed. More than insults or mockery, what she couldn't stand was being ignored.

"Do you want me to mock you? Is that it?" Raquel insisted.

He lowered the bottle and faced her without saying a word. They stood a meter apart, testing each other, waiting to see who would give in first. It was a game they played so often that no one else paid any attention. Silently, with a raised chin, he signaled Raquel to show her hand. She smirked.

"How does it feel to get your ass fucked by Pitito?" she spat, arms akimbo. "There you go. Is that what you wanted?"

Benteveo said nothing, just pressed the glass bottle against Raquel's chest and pushed. She endured the pain and held his gaze, then grabbed him roughly and turned him to face her. The brutal, firm knee struck Benteveo's unprotected groin, leaving him doubled over on the floor.

"Remember, I'm not one of El Ruso's little whores, you asshole."

Accustomed to shouting and numbed by the blaring cumbia music they listened to every day, the young people living next door didn't hear a thing. Not when the beer bottle shattered against the kitchen door, nor when Raquel slammed into the fridge after taking a punch to the face.

"Did you split my lip?" Raquel exclaimed, feeling the blood running down her chin with her fingers. "Did you split my lip, you fat jerk?"

Even though he knew it wasn't the best course of action, Benteveo smirked.

"Is this funny to you?" Raquel grabbed the fireplace poker and advanced toward Benteveo. "Just wait until I tell everyone you're a faggot."

Seeing the iron instrument nearly upon him, Benteveo recoiled and fell backward onto the bed.

Raquel couldn't remember how many times she had told him she hated that he slept with a gun under the pillow. "Stop with the Hollywood cop dramas; it'll go off while we're sleeping," she had said the last time. But the response was always the same, "You know I can't sleep a wink if I don't have it there."

Benteveo fired two shots almost simultaneously, and the poker whistled past his head by mere centimeters.

XXII

The reverse display case glowed at night when the office was only illuminated by the streetlights. From there, through the large windows overlooking Rodó Park, one could observe the neighborhood's life in detail, though it was rare for those who worked there to have time to look outside. However, this was Pitito's favorite pastime when he stayed after hours. The upcoming election day had made him familiar with the routines of some locals, whom he now watched with obsessive care. So much so that when he saw the limping lady taking her poodle for a walk, he knew he had to start wrapping up to get some sleep.

He returned to his laptop screen and went over the same three paragraphs of the speech for the committee once more. It was the fifth time he had read them, and he couldn't retain a single idea. And while the event was very important ("they all are," Mariño would have corrected him), the interview he had scheduled with Aguirre first thing in the morning was the only thing occupying his mind.

He got up and walked around the meeting table, searching for the willpower he had lost. He looked out the window and saw the lady and her old poodle heading back. Pitito sighed and slammed his laptop shut.

"Screw it. I'll wing it."

"That's exactly what you're worst at," a voice emerged from the darkness of the large common room.

Pitito froze, afraid to breathe.

"Who's there? Don't make me call the police," he finally dared.

A spontaneous laugh followed by a stubborn cough gave away the stranger.

"What are you doing here?" Pitito stepped into the darkness, grabbed Benteveo by the shirt, and pulled him into the dim light where he could see him. "Why were you hiding there?"

Benteveo freed himself from the grip and pushed him away with friendly roughness.

"I wanted to see how long it would take you to notice," he replied, adjusting his shirt. "You're rusty."

Pitito ignored him and went into the fishbowl to fetch his jacket.

"Wanna go grab a beer?"

"Depends on you."

Not fully understanding, Pitito headed for the door, patting his pockets in search of the office key.

"Alright, let's go then," he ordered.

Benteveo, calm and with careful movements, positioned himself in front of him, blocking his way to the exit.

"If you realize how things are and cancel that interview, we can go for a beer," he announced, eyes fixed on the carpet and fists clenched inside his leather jacket pockets.

Pitito instinctively took a step back. The second step was deliberate, knowing the conversation would take a while, and neither wanted to have it in public. Carefully, Pitito left his jacket folded on one of the chairs in the waiting room and invited Benteveo to sit down.

"We're getting old, Bente," he said as he took a seat in a leather chair. "It's time to think about how we want to spend the few years we have left."

Benteveo stood firm, barely turning his gaze to address Pitito.

"Stop with the millennial nonsense. I've had enough of covering for your mess."

"Which one are you talking about?" Pitito retorted, smiling at the joke.

However, the intense look Benteveo gave him was all he needed to understand what he meant. The adrenaline rush hit him hard.

"Oh, Benteveo... why?" Pitito exclaimed, rubbing his forehead as he searched for the right words. "It's not what you think. I never mentioned you."

Immobile, like a mannequin from a Fall-Winter collection for 60-year-olds, Benteveo remained silent. From his seat, Pitito looked at him, unsure of what to do. Against all odds, he stood up and caressed Benteveo's cheek.

"You're an idiot..."

Pitito's kiss was tender but passionate, as if it had been held back for a long time. Benteveo's initially cold lips gradually softened, and his hands gripped Pitito's back firmly. Pitito smiled and slid his tongue into Benteveo's mouth. Between gasps, he unbuckled his belt and removed his pants. He struggled to pull down his black briefs, revealing his erection. Benteveo suddenly stepped back.

"Benteveo, I love you."

"That's why."

The building's walls echoed with the gunshot. Pitito, in disbelief and spasming, clutched his stomach as if waiting for an explanation. He collapsed, trying to speak as Benteveo walked away without looking back.

XXIII

Facing each other in silence like a standoff, the three remained motionless since the Astute had entered the apartment. Carolina regretted imagining how her mother would react when she found out she had been murdered, and every breath was a small victory that prolonged the agony. Benteveo watched both of them, burdened by the uncertainty of solving the mess without having to kill the only friend he had left. The Astute, on the other hand, was lost in a melancholic anger, and his calm demeanor made it seem like he was unaware of what was happening.

"The Ruso... Pitito," he mumbled, on the verge of breaking down.

There was no response.

"Raquel too?" the Astute asked innocently.

Benteveo looked him in the eyes and pulled out the gun he had tucked in his pants. Carolina clenched her fists, bracing for the worst.

"I don't know what right you think you have. But just because we're friends doesn't mean I owe you any explanation."

"We're not friends," the Astute declared.

"Alright then."

The shot pierced his chest, shattering the vintage lamp Carolina had bought online just two weeks ago. The impact knocked him down, and he writhed in pain for a few seconds before taking his last breath. The Astute's hand trembled, gripping the gun as if his life depended on it.

"You always told me to carry a gun," he whispered.

EPILOGUE

I

Five minutes before the presentation was set to begin, the room was a dazzling array of empty chairs. The complete series on DVD, along with the book compiling the transcripts of all the interviews, was the producers' last-ditch effort to recoup at least part of their investment in what had turned out to be an economic failure.

Despite the lackluster impact of the documentary series, Carolina felt she had managed to convey what she wanted. Even though "Aftermath of the Guerrilla" hadn't garnered the expected awards or generated much interest—since the Tupamaros were slowly fading from public consciousness—she found a niche in her profession that allowed her to wake up and work almost without suffering. She couldn't call it a "vocation" because she didn't believe in that; it was simply something she could tolerate to make a living.

The small hall in the community center of Colonia del Sacramento could accommodate up to 50 people, but only seven were present. Carolina wasn't surprised. She took a deep breath, exchanged glances with Peti and Lechón, and took the microphone to begin.

As part of the promotion, the producers had insisted that one of the interviewed Tupamaros attend the presentations. After the media frenzy that followed the murders the previous year, they desperately wanted the Astute. Carolina didn't protest, not even when tasked with extending the invitation, knowing in advance what the outcome would be. The same thing had happened months earlier when she tried to contact him to check on him: the phone was disconnected, and the apartment had been vacant for weeks. None of the other former Tupamaros who knew him had heard from him in a long time. When her interest turned from curiosity to concern, Carolina even tried tracking down El Ruso's mother, only to discover she had died not long after her son. On a whim, she wandered through bars he used to frequent, but there was no trace of the Astute.

She cleared her throat and glanced one last time at the outline of topics she wanted to cover. Carolina's words echoed among the empty chairs as she remembered the talk she had given at the university a few weeks ago. One of the present Tupamaros (she couldn't recall his nickname now) had been asked about the Astute's disappearance and had explained it better than anyone: "It was the world that disappeared for him. He had no one left, only memories."

II

The blonde wig was made for a much smaller head and seemed to squeeze his skull every time he opened his mouth. The mustache was real and meticulously groomed. However, the star of the ensemble was the light brown bottle-bottom glasses he wore. Behind the lenses, his eyes appeared so tiny they seemed disconnected from his face.

"If I had known I'd see you like this, I would've asked Pepe to leave me here from the start," the Astute commented quietly across the table.

"Looks like spending so much time among common prisoners has left you a bit dazed."

They shook hands, and El Ruso pulled him in for a strong hug, patting his back several times until he softened.

"Alright, alright, break it up!" the guard's voice called

from his desk.

It was the first visit the Astute had received since the escape. A year and a half had passed since that night when most of his comrades—and all his friends—had fled through a tunnel. Since then, many were back in cells, now in the brand-new Libertad Prison. The Astute had no close family, and since the emergency security measures, his lawyer had stopped answering his calls. For someone who prided himself on being prepared for anything inside the prison, nothing was more unexpected than this visit. It was a huge risk for just a few minutes of conversation and the chance to smuggle something. Then again, El Ruso had always liked betting on the losing side.

"How are you holding up?" he asked, concerned.

The Astute shrugged.

"Things aren't much better out there. The places I've had to hide in, sometimes I think I'd rather be inside."

In less than three minutes, he caught him up on the situation of their closest allies, shared some news that didn't make it into the papers, and gave him the contact for a new lawyer who could help him.

"Lechón sends you regards. He wanted to come, but

it's best if you don't have many visitors, to dissociate yourself from the escapees. But I had to bring you this."

El Ruso lunged across the table and hugged him again. The guard saw and cleared his throat loudly. A package subtly slipped into the pocket of the oversized jacket the Astute was wearing.

"What's this?" he exclaimed, feeling the nearly half-kilo bag of dulce de leche now hanging by his leg.

"Just keep it hidden," urged El Ruso. "Try it later; you'll see it tastes better in here."

The Astute laughed and managed to say only "thanks," when he should have given him a hug, one of the many he owed him.

ABOUT THE AUTHOR

Pablo Leguísamo

Pablo Leguísamo, known as Roy in the comic world, holds a degree in Advertising Communication and is a writer and screenwriter for film and television. His notable works include From the Little Field to the Final, The Pérez Family Travels to Mars, Dying for El Che, Tupamaros, The Escape, and Of Milk, Sweet. He won the 2012 Graphic Novel contest by Montevideo Comic for his work The Bad Parts and the 2016 Banda Dibujada award in the category of "Non-fiction Comic Book for Young Adults" for Tupamaros, The Escape.

Made in the USA
Columbia, SC
27 December 2024